RIDIN' THAT
STRAWBERRY ROAN

Illustrated by Marcia Sewall

PUFFIN BOOKS

PUFFIN BOOKS
Viking Penguin Inc., 40 West 23rd Street, New York, New York 10010, U.S.A.
Penguin Books Ltd, Harmondsworth, Middlesex, England
Penguin Books Australia Ltd, Ringwood, Victoria, Australia
Penguin Books Canada Limited,
2801 John Street, Markham, Ontario, Canada L3R 1B4
Penguin Books (N.Z.) Ltd,
182–190 Wairau Road, Auckland 10, New Zealand

First published by Viking Penguin Inc. 1985
Published in Picture Puffins 1987
Copyright © Marcia Sewall, 1985
All rights reserved
Printed in Japan by Dai Nippon Printing Company Ltd.
Set in Bookman Light

Library of Congress Cataloging in Publication Data
Sewall, Marcia.   Ridin' that strawberry roan.
Reprint. Originally published: New York, N.Y.: Viking Kestrel, 1985.
Summary: Follows the adventures of a brave but foolhardy bronco buster
as he meets his match in the horse called "Strawberry Roan."
Based on an old Western folksong.
[1. Cowboys—Fiction.   2. Horses—Fiction.   3. West (U.S.)—Fiction.
4. Stories in rhyme]   I. Title.   [PZ8.3.S479Ri   1987]   [E]
86-25474   ISBN 0-14-050722-1

For Uncle Rufus,
my favorite storyteller

Well, I'm standin' 'round town just a-wastin' my time.
I'm out of a job and I ain't got a dime,

When this old boy steps up, and he says, "I suppose
That you're a bronc-rider by the rig of your clothes."

He guesses me right, that's my middle name.
"Have you got a bad horse that you're aimin' to tame?
'Cause a horse never lived, nor never drew breath

That I couldn't ride till he starved plum to death!"
He says, "Git your saddle, I'll give you a chance."
We hop in the buckboard and boil to the ranch.

Down in the horse corral a-standin' alone
Is a little old horse, just a strawberry roan.
He's U-necked and old, with a long lower jaw,

You can see with one eye he's a real outlaw horse.
His legs is all spavined, he's got pigeon toes,
Little pin eyes, and a long Roman nose.

So, I puts on my spurs and I fix up my twine.
I stick on my hat and I'm sure feeling fine.
I throw a loop on him and it's well I know then,
That before I git aboard him I'll sure earn my ten!

Next come the blinds and they were a real fight.
On goes my saddle and I screws her down tight.
Then I git aboard him and I raises the blinds

And I takes a deep seat just to feel him unwind.
First he bows his old head then he leaps from the ground.
Twenty circles he makes before coming down.

He's the worst bronco I've seen on the range.
He'll land on a nickel and give you the change.

And while he's a-buckin' he squeals like a shoat.
I tell you that pony has sure got my goat.

He goes up in the east, he comes down in the west.
To stay in his middle I'm doin' my best.

Then he takes a big jump and he spins at the top.
I ask him politely, "Oh, horse, won't you stop?"

Way up at the top of each stiff-legged buck,
He sucks himself back and you're ridin' on luck!

He turns his old belly right up to the sun.
He says, "Hang on, cowboy, I'll show you some fun!"

My reins is all broke and my bit's hangin' loose.

My saddle is slippin' back on his caboose.

Then he turns inside out and he swallers his hide,
And that was the end, boys, of my ten-dollar ride.

Well, first I go north, and then I go west,
Just hunting the place where I can find rest.

Then I turn over twice and I come back to earth
And I sets there a-cussin' the day of his birth.

And I says, "There's some horses that I cannot ride.

There's some of them livin', boys, they haven't all died!"